THE

ENCHANTED TUNNEL

— BOOK THREE —

JOURNEY TO JERUSALEM

THE ENCHANTED TUNNEL

BOOK THREE
JOURNEY TO JERUSALEM

Marianne Monson

Illustrated by Dan Burr

DESERET
BOOK

SALT LAKE CITY, UTAH

Library of Congress Cataloging-in-Publication Data

Monson, Marianne, 1975– author.
   Journey to Jerusalem / Marianne Monson ; illustrated by Dan Burr.
       p. cm. — (Enchanted tunnel ; book three)
   Summary: Aria and Nathan return to the Enchanted Tunnel, and find
themselves in Jerusalem at the time of Christ.
   ISBN 978-1-60908-068-6 (paperbound)
   1. Space and time—Juvenile fiction.   2. Jesus Christ—Juvenile fiction.
3. Jerusalem—Juvenile fiction.   4. Brothers and sisters—Juvenile fiction.
5. Mormons—Juvenile fiction.   6. Children's stories. [1. Space and
time—Fiction.   2. Jesus Christ—Fiction.   3. Jerusalem—Fiction.
4. Brothers and sisters—Fiction.   5. Mormons—Fiction.
6. Twins—Fiction.]   I. Burr, Dan, 1951– illustrator.   II. Title.   III. Series:
Monson, Marianne, 1975– Enchanted tunnel ; book three.
   PZ7.M76282Jou 2011
   [Fic]—dc22   2010048977

Printed in the United States of America
Malloy Lithographing Incorporated, Ann Arbor, MI

10   9   8   7   6   5   4   3   2   1

For my parents,
Dwight and Marilynn,
who journeyed to Jerusalem with me

A BIG THANK-YOU

Special thanks to Professor Brent L. Top of Brigham Young University for leading me through Jerusalem as a student and for graciously sharing his knowledge of the New Testament for this book.

A NOTE TO THE READER

When I read a good book, I like to know if it *really* happened. The Enchanted Tunnel books are historical fiction, which means that part of the book is true and part is made up. Nathan and Aria and their adventures in the enchanted tunnel are imagined.

But the information that comes from the scriptures and church history is absolutely true. It *really* happened. We know about these events from the scriptures, pioneer journals, and historical records. Some of the details, such as what the characters were eating or doing on a specific day, are invented, but only after learning about the types of things they *often* did.

When I was a child, I sometimes found it

difficult to relate to people in the scriptures who lived long ago. Luckily, I had teachers and parents who brought the scriptures to life. These teachers opened a magic tunnel in my mind that helped me imagine myself in the story. It is my hope that the Enchanted Tunnel books will do the same for you.

1

HARD WORK

"Ouch!" said Aria. She dropped the needle and sucked on her finger.

"We can trade jobs, if you want," said Nathan. He was standing by the sink in the laundry room, scrubbing a pioneer dress with a toothbrush.

"That's okay," said Aria, picking up the needle again. "We have to learn to do these chores ourselves sometime."

"But we're not used to doing our own laundry," said Nathan. "I don't know if I've ever seen Mom so mad."

Aria pulled the needle through the fabric of a faded pioneer bonnet and smiled. "The clothes we bought the other day will be perfect for wearing in the tunnel, but next time I hope we don't have to run from any soldiers."

"I thought it was fun!" said Nathan, remembering their narrow escape from their previous adventure.

A few minutes later Aria said, "That's the last hole. It's ready for the washing machine."

"I've scrubbed all the stains," said Nathan. "They should pass even Mom's inspection."

They put laundry detergent in the washing machine, added the clothes, and turned it on. An hour later the clothes were washed and dried. They pulled them from the warm dryer, and Mom came to check.

"How do they look?" she asked.

They held up the costumes, and she looked pleased. "You did a good job," she said. "Now you just have to iron them."

"What?" Nathan whined. "I hate ironing.

They weren't ironed at the church. They were just stuffed in a box."

"Then you can leave them better than you found them," said Mom with a smile. "Except for the patches."

Nathan sighed and turned on the iron while Aria set up the ironing board. Nathan pretended that the wrinkles were Pharaoh's soldiers as he flattened them with the iron. "Take that!" he said.

Twenty minutes later, Aria said, "We're finally done."

"Hey," said Nathan. "Tonight is Tuesday. The church will be open for Young Men's. Let's take the costumes back to the church right now." He nudged Aria.

"Great," said Aria. "I'll get the used clothes we bought."

"I'll grab my scripture bag!" said Nathan.

2

RETURN WHAT YOU BORROW

"I don't see why you have to take them back tonight," said Mom. "Sunday will be fine."

"You always say to return something you borrow as quickly as possible," said Aria.

Nathan nodded. "Besides, what if they need them for the Young Men activity?"

"Hmmm," said Mom. "That doesn't seem very likely." She looked from one eager face to the other. "Oh, all right, but hurry home. You still have homework to do."

"We will!" said Aria.

They folded the costumes carefully and put them into a sack. Aria went to her room and got the clothes they had bought from a thrift store with allowance money. "Tunnel clothes,"

Nathan called them. Mom couldn't get mad if those clothes got dirty. Aria went back to the kitchen where Nathan was waiting with his scripture bag.

"Let's go!" he said.

They ran across the street to the church. The side door was open, and they heard teenagers talking in the hall. They waved to Jennifer Andrus, a girl who watched them sometimes when their mom wasn't home, and then darted around the corner.

"What if someone's in the gym?" asked Aria.

Nathan shrugged. They opened the doors and Nathan peeked inside. "The coast is clear!" he said.

They climbed up on the stage and returned the folded church costumes to the box.

Aria pulled her second-hand dress from the sack and stepped behind the covered wagon scenery to change. She zipped up the dress and stepped onto the stage. "How do I look?"

"Like Mary from the Christmas play," said Nathan.

"Yeah," said Aria. "It's true." Her dress was made from brown fabric and probably had been a costume from a Christmas play. "I thought it would work for most places the tunnel would take us. I can't really bring a whole bunch of different outfits, you know."

"That's why I'm glad I'm a boy," said Nathan. He was wearing brown pants and a blue, old-fashioned shirt. He held up a piece of beige fabric. "But I got this just in case we end up someplace where the boys are all wearing dresses again."

"They weren't dresses," said Aria.

"They looked like dresses to me," said Nathan. "Come on!"

Aria tied on the pioneer bonnet she had bought. "Okay," she said.

They hopped off the stage and opened the door to one of the storage cupboards under the stage. It was filled with a rack of metal chairs.

"Uh-oh," said Nathan. "I forgot that the chairs wouldn't be set up for church."

"They look really heavy," said Aria.

"We can move them," said Nathan. He grabbed the end of the rack and started pulling.

Aria reached for the other end and tugged. The rack moved a couple of inches. They pulled again. "Yikes," said Aria. "They are *heavy*."

Inch by inch, they dragged the rack into the middle of the gym. By the time they got it into the center of the floor, they were both breathing hard.

"Should we just leave it there?" asked Aria.

"It will seem like we're only gone for a minute, right?" said Nathan.

"I think so," said Aria.

"Then let's go!"

3

A BROKEN TUNNEL

They darted into the tunnel and started crawling. The concrete was cold and smooth beneath Nathan's hands. He couldn't wait to see where they were going to end up this time.

The tunnel was even darker than he remembered. Nathan searched ahead for light, but all he saw was blackness. They crawled for a few minutes in the darkness.

"Ouch!" Nathan said, as his head bashed into something hard.

Aria crashed into him from behind. "Oww!" she said. "What's the matter? Why did you stop?"

"It's the end of the wall," said Nathan. He

rubbed his head. It felt like he was going to have a goose bump.

"What happened?" said Aria.

"I don't know," said Nathan. "It didn't work."

"Uh-oh," said Aria. She slid her hand along the wall. It was definitely cold, hard concrete.

"Why isn't it working?" said Nathan, starting to get upset.

Aria shrugged. "Do you think the magic works only on Sundays?"

"Maybe."

"Mom is going to get mad if we don't come back soon," said Aria.

Nathan unzipped his scripture bag and pulled out his flashlight. The light made strange shadows around the tunnel.

"We need to think about what makes the magic work," said Aria. "What did we do before that we aren't doing now?"

"Did we say anything special?"

The wall sure *looked* solid. Aria pushed on it. "All the other times there was a tingling feeling, like electricity," she said.

"But how do we make that happen?" asked Nathan.

Aria shrugged.

A few minutes later, they crawled out of the tunnel and sat in front of the storage door, dusty and discouraged.

"I feel like it was all a dream," said Aria.

"It wasn't a dream," said Nathan. "You have pioneer beads sitting in your room at home, silly."

"I know," said Aria. "But it's so amazing, just like a dream. I want to go back again and again and again."

"Yeah," said Nathan.

"There has to be something we're missing,"

said Aria. "Something that made the magic work before."

"The first time we went through the tunnel you were chasing me," said Nathan. "You were trying to get the M&M's back, and you were wearing that silly bonnet."

"That's right!" said Aria. "I was wearing the pioneer bonnet. Maybe that is part of the magic!"

"It's worth trying," said Nathan, jumping up. He climbed up on the stage and pulled the old bonnet out of the costume box. Then he jumped off the stage and handed it to Aria.

"I really hope this works," she said.

"Should I hold some peanut M&M's in my hand, just in case?" said Nathan.

"No," said Aria, laughing. "I have never heard of magic M&M's."

"I've never heard of a magic bonnet either," said Nathan in a grumpy voice.

Aria untied the new bonnet and left it on the stage. She tugged on the old bonnet and followed Nathan into the tunnel. As soon as Aria knelt down, an electric shock sizzled along the ground.

"Did you feel that?" asked Nathan.

"Yes!" said Aria. They crawled through the darkness until the ground under their hands and knees didn't feel like concrete anymore. Rocks and dirt lined the bottom of the tunnel, which opened up to a low cave.

At the end of the tunnel, Nathan spied a glimmer of light. "Here we go!" he said.

4

DAMASCUS GATE

The cave entrance was a narrow slit of light. From outside the entrance, they heard noise. It sounded like a hundred people calling to each other—everyone was talking, arguing, and laughing all at once.

Aria peeked around the corner. "Uh-oh," she said.

"What?" asked Nathan, trying to see over her shoulder.

"I'm not going to need the pioneer bonnet," said Aria. She tugged at the strings and pulled it off.

"Be careful," said Nathan. "Now we know we can't get home without that."

"Let's put it in your scripture bag," said Aria.

She stuffed the bonnet in the bag and zipped it shut.

Nathan peeked around the corner of the cave. "Wow!" he said. "Is that a castle?"

"I don't know," said Aria. She looked again. They were standing in front of a high stone wall with pointed tops. Long steps led down to an enormous gate. Crowds of people filled the square. Some people were crowded around the entrance to the gate. Others traveled along the road. Shopkeepers stood next to tables.

"*Dahuf!*" they heard someone shout.

"*Ma shlomkha?*"

It was a messy jumble of people—all speaking languages they didn't understand.

"Rats, they're wearing dresses again," Nathan said. He pulled out the beige piece of fabric he had brought and draped it over one shoulder.

"And the women all have scarves on their

heads," said Aria. "Will they notice that I don't have one?"

"Only one way to find out!" said Nathan. He left the cave and walked into the middle of the street, pulling Aria behind him.

The shouting was louder now. People rushed by in every direction. A man pushed a cart piled high with bread. Another man seemed to be arguing about the price of cabbages. A woman with a bright green scarf sat on the ground, surrounded by baskets of vegetables.

"Look," said Aria, pointing. "Leeks."

"No, thanks," said Nathan, making a disgusted face.

A little girl with braided hair carried a basket filled with fluffy baby chicks. "Awww," said Aria.

"Kama ze ole," yelled a man.

"We can't understand them," said Aria.

Nathan suddenly thought of something. "When we were in Egypt, we couldn't understand anyone until we turned on the GPS." Nathan moved out of the way of a man leading a donkey. He unzipped his scripture bag and pulled out his GPS. "Maybe . . ."

"*Zuz! Zuz!*" a man called, waving his arms in the air. Nathan turned on the GPS and waited for it to load. "Move out of the way!" the man said.

Nathan and Aria ran out of his way. "That's better," said Aria.

Nathan frowned after the man. "I think I liked it better when I couldn't understand him," he said.

"Hello!" called a woman selling vegetables. "Special price for you today!"

"Where are we?" asked Aria.

Nathan looked at his GPS system. "It says, 'Damascus Gate, Jerusalem,'" said Nathan.

"*Jerusalem?*" said Aria. "Nathan! We're in Jerusalem!"

"That's what I just said."

"Let's go see it, then!" said Aria. She turned and walked down the wide steps toward the gate of the city. A sign on the stone wall said "Damascus Gate."

"Wait up!" called Nathan, running after her.

5

SCARVES FOR M&M'S

Aria passed under the tall stone arch of Damascus Gate and found herself on a narrow street that twisted and turned. Other streets and passageways branched off in every direction.

"Aria!" panted Nathan, as he caught up to her. "Where are you going?"

"Exploring," said Aria.

She was dazzled by the sights, sounds, and smells of the city. The ancient-looking walls were made from light chiseled stone. The children passed an arch hung with metal lanterns. Their shoes clattered on the flat stone streets.

On either side of the street, shopkeepers invited them into their stores.

"Special price for you, Miss!"

"Come this way!"

Some of the shops sold vegetables stacked high in colorful piles—cucumbers, leeks, olives, and figs. Other shops sold purses and bags made from leather.

"Take a look!" called a man selling pottery.

Aria turned down a side street. The street wound back and forth and split into three different paths.

"How are we ever going to find our way back?" said Nathan. "This place is like a maze."

Aria shrugged. "We'll figure it out." She sniffed the air. "Mmmm, spices." One of the shops had baskets filled with herbs, as well as scarves hanging on hooks and beautifully embroidered dresses. Aria stopped and touched one of the hanging scarves. It was orange with a gold pattern.

"I give you a good deal, Miss," said the shopkeeper.

"All the other girls are wearing scarves," said Aria. "Maybe I should wear one too."

"But we don't have any money," said Nathan.

"You don't need money," said the shopkeeper. "You can trade. What do you have?"

Aria unzipped Nathan's scripture bag. They needed the flashlight and GPS unit. Water. Snacks. Hmmm. She held up a package of peanut M&M's. "Would you take this?" she asked.

The shopkeeper looked surprised. "What is this?"

"It's candy," said Nathan. The shopkeeper looked confused. Nathan tore off one end of the package and dropped an M&M into the shopkeeper's hand.

The shopkeeper put it in his mouth. His eyes widened in surprise. "Delicious," he said.

Aria poured the rest of the candy into a small jar.

The shopkeeper lifted the orange scarf off the hook and handed it to Aria. She smiled and wound the scarf over her hair. "Thank you!" she said.

As they walked away, they noticed the shopkeeper showing his friend the M&M's.

"I hope he enjoys those," said Nathan. "Something tells me he's never going to taste anything like them again."

Aria giggled.

6

A JERUSALEM SNACK

"What is that smell?" said Nathan.

"Yum," said Aria. "It smells like bread baking!"

A nearby shop had an oven built into the wall. Red-hot coals burned at the back of the oven, and round circles of bread dough baked inside. The bread puffed up in the middle as it baked. It smelled fantastic, and several people stood in line, waiting for the bread to finish baking.

Nathan and Aria stopped to watch. The heat from the oven warmed them like a miniature sun.

An older boy also waited in line. He turned around and smiled at them. Aria felt a flicker of recognition. Had she seen that boy some-where before?

After a few minutes, the circles of bread turned golden brown. The baker took a wooden paddle from the shelf and reached into the stone oven. With a flick of his wrist, he scooped up the circles of bread with the paddle and pulled them out of the oven. He dropped them onto a wooden rack to cool.

"Passover is over," the shopkeeper an-nounced. "Time for fresh, hot pita again!" He took six pieces and wrapped them in paper. He handed the packages to the people waiting in line. They each dropped a coin into a cup on the counter.

The boy was last in line. He took his pack-age of pita and turned toward Nathan and Aria. "I'm Yeshua," he said. "Would you like some pita?"

Aria looked at Nathan. The boy had dark

brown hair and kind, gentle eyes. *I would trust him with anything,* Aria thought. She wondered again why he seemed so familiar.

Nathan looked at the pita. "Sure," he said.

Yeshua handed Aria a piece of pita bread. It was warm from the oven and still puffed with steamy air. When she took the first bite, warm air escaped like a sigh. It was crisp on the outside and chewy in the middle. "Wow," said Aria. "It's delicious."

Nathan nodded happily, for the boy had given him one too. "Aren't you going to eat one?" Nathan asked.

The boy nodded and bit into another pita. He wrapped up the rest. "I'm saving this for a friend," he said.

The boy slipped the bread into a bag he was carrying. As he told them good-bye, his warm eyes held theirs in a way that made them feel as if they had seen him many times before. Then he waved and set off down the street.

"That boy looked familiar to me," said Aria.

"That's funny. I thought so too," said Nathan.

"I can't remember who he reminds me of," said Aria. She tapped her finger on her chin, looking after him. "Come on," she said at last. "Let's see where he's going."

"Okay," said Nathan, as Aria darted in the direction the boy had gone.

7

HELPING A FRIEND

The boy had disappeared. Aria thought she saw a flash of his robe as he turned another corner. They raced after him, trying to catch another glimpse. Aria gasped for breath.

When they got to the end of the street, it was empty.

"We lost him," said Aria.

"No, look!" said Nathan, pointing. The boy had turned down a twisting side street. Nathan caught a view of him before he vanished again.

They followed after the boy, being careful not to get too close. He seemed to know the streets well. To Aria and Nathan, the stone passageways seemed impossible to keep straight.

They were getting closer. Suddenly the

street opened up to a crowded plaza. Carts loaded with supplies rumbled past. People carried baskets filled with items to sell or buy. The walls of a huge stone palace rose above the plaza.

"Did we lose him?" asked Nathan. The boy had melted into the crowd.

Aria searched the plaza. It was a jumble of faces and fabrics. They would never find him now.

She gazed along the edges of the square. Suddenly she said, "Look!"

There, in a dark corner, a man dressed in dirty, ragged clothes slumped on the ground. A crutch lay next to his twisted leg. He was begging for money from the people passing by.

Sitting in front of the man was the boy they had followed. Yeshua handed the man pita bread. They talked and smiled. It looked like the man had not smiled in a long time.

"He said the pita was for a friend," said Aria.

"I guess that's his friend," said Nathan.

"That man could use a friend," said Aria thoughtfully. She noticed all the well-dressed people hurrying by. No one else seemed to notice the boy feeding the hungry man. The man ate eagerly, and Aira felt tears coming to her eyes. If they hadn't been following the boy, would she have noticed the man and helped him? Or would she have rushed by like everyone else?

The man finished eating, and Yeshua gave him a smile. Then the boy turned and started walking up the large stairway.

"Come on," said Nathan. "He's going up."

They ran across the plaza and started to climb the enormous stone staircase. It was the largest staircase either of them had ever seen. As they climbed higher, they could see the city of Jerusalem spread out below.

Roman guards wearing red tunics stood at the bend of the staircase, and their metal armor flashed in the sun.

"Cool," said Nathan. "Look at their swords."

"No, thanks," said Aria, thinking of Egypt. She didn't want to be chased by any more soldiers. She walked by on the other side of the stairs.

At the top, the staircase turned and continued upward, right into the huge palace lined with columns. More guards stood outside the palace, although these guards looked more like priests than soldiers.

Yeshua turned and continued climbing.

"I'm tired," said Aria. "This is a lot of stairs!"

Nathan stopped. "Should we still follow him? I don't know if we can go into that palace or not."

Aria looked at the other people entering. "Everyone else is, so I guess it's probably okay.

Look, other kids are going in," she said, pointing.

"All right," said Nathan, "but if one of those guards comes after us, don't blame me!"

Aria looked warily at the guards. They stood like statues.

The children started up the last enormous set of steps. They were both breathing hard by the time they got to the top. The palace walls seemed to reach into the sky. At the top of the gate was a statue of a golden eagle. They passed through the gate and found a long hallway lined with pillars. Beyond the pillars was a vast courtyard.

All the people in the courtyard wore something on their heads—the women wore scarves of many different colors, and all the men wore white shawls with fringe on the ends. Most of the men also wore black leather boxes on their foreheads. "What are those?" Nathan asked.

"I don't know," said Aria.

Yeshua had disappeared again. In the middle of the courtyard, a dazzling white building glistened in the sun. Gold decorations covered the top, and golden pillars gleamed. A smaller stone wall ran around the outside, and a spiral of smoke curled slowly skyward in front of the building.

"Wait a minute," Aria gasped. "I don't think this is a palace."

8

HOUSE OF THE LORD

"What is it, then?" asked Nathan.

"This must be the temple!" said Aria. "The ancient temple of Jerusalem! See the smoke? That must be coming from the altar."

"You mean where they kill animals?"

"Yes, like during Passover. Look—that woman is carrying a basket with a bird inside it," she pointed out.

"Poor birdy," said Nathan.

Aria nodded.

They walked across the vast courtyard to the temple. A low wall ran around the temple and signs were posted on it. Aria read, "Israelites only. No foreigner is to enter within the balustrade and enclosure around the temple area.

Whoever is caught will have himself to blame for his death, which will follow."

"I'm not going in there!" said Nathan.

"But you *are* an Israelite, silly," said Aria.

"I am?"

"Yes, don't you remember that Brother King told us we are children of Israel?" said Aria. Brother King was the children's Primary teacher, who frequently challenged them to research answers to the questions they so often had. "Some of these people could be our own ancestors!"

"But do *they* know that?" said Nathan.

Aria shrugged and walked forward.

"It says 'death,'" pointed out Nathan.

"I *am* an Israelite!" said Aria. Nathan trailed after her.

"More stairs," groaned Nathan.

"Up, up, up to the temple," said Aria. They climbed the short staircase that led to another stone wall. The huge doorways were carved with decorations of silver and gold.

"Wow," said Nathan, as they passed through the gates. Inside was another courtyard. Many of the people inside were praying as they faced the temple. Others carried animals to be sacrificed. Priests, dressed in white robes, moved across the courtyard, talking to people.

In one corner stood a group of musicians playing instruments the children had never seen before. The instruments looked like fancy harps and flutes, thought Aria. A few priests stood next to the musicians who were singing. Some people were even dancing. It was a reverent kind of dance.

Aria moved closer to hear the song. The music was beautiful. She tried to listen to the words. "Who shall stand in the Lord's holy place?" they sang. "He who has clean hands

and a pure heart." The music floated through the air like a reverent, joyful hymn.

At the other end of the courtyard, more stairs led up to a bronze gate, where only priests seemed to be going.

Above the bronze gate, the white marble of the temple rose into the sky. The building towered above them. They could hear animals bleating and see smoke rising from a wide altar.

"It doesn't smell very good," Nathan whispered.

"Shhh," said Aria. "It's because they are offering animal sacrifices. It's sacred, like the sacrament."

Aria looked at the faces of the people praying. They looked so sincere, so grateful to be at the temple. She wondered how far they had traveled to be there.

"Look," said Aria. "The white marble looks like the stone on the temple near our house."

Nathan nodded. "The building reminds me of the temple."

"That's because it *is* a temple, silly," said Aria.

Nathan nodded. "Let's go," he said, "before someone asks us to prove that we're Israelites."

9

A BOY TEACHING

They walked down the stone steps and past the wall with signs. Aria felt as though she werc climbing back down to earth after being in heaven.

As they walked across the enormous courtyard, she looked at the faces of the people. Men, women, children, old, young, handsome, plain—they had all come to worship God at the temple. She looked for the boy from the city, but he had disappeared.

They passed through the rows of columns, which seemed to go on forever. As they walked between the columns, Nathan noticed a group of people sitting on cushions. There were priests and other men with fancy hats and robes. In the center of the group sat a boy.

"Look!" said Nathan.

Aria turned. "It's Yeshua!" she said. They moved closer. The group was sitting in the shade under the columns. They were talking excitedly, and one of the priests gestured with his hands.

The people were asking the boy questions. He answered calmly and didn't seem nervous. His eyes were calm and kind.

Nathan and Aria moved closer. The boy saw them and smiled. They sat down at the edge of the group. A few priests glanced in their direction but said nothing.

"The greatest commandment," Yeshua was saying, "is to love the Lord thy God with all thy heart, might, mind and strength. And the second is to love thy neighbor as thyself."

The priests seemed shocked by his answer. They discussed his words among themselves.

"What rabbi has taught you this?" one asked him.

The boy replied, "My Father taught me."

Some of the priests nodded; others shook their heads.

But the boy did not seem to be concerned. "This is the meaning of all the law and the prophets," he said. "Love God, and love all men."

As Aria listened to his words, her body burned with warmth, just like when she had stood next to the stone oven. She couldn't remember ever feeling the Spirit so strongly before. At last she remembered a story from the New Testament, and she knew why the boy had looked so familiar.

"Nathan," she whispered, her eyes filling rapidly with tears.

"What?"

"Do you know who he is?"

Nathan nodded, and Aria saw that his eyes too were wet.

Aria smiled. They listened to Jesus talk about sacrifice and the Passover and the temple. He spoke of the scriptures, and they had never before seemed so simple and clear. Nathan and Aria were amazed by his understanding when the priests and Pharisees asked him questions. They felt that they never wanted to leave.

"You are only a boy, not yet a son of the commandment," said one Pharisee. "How can one so young know this?"

Aria looked at the temple. *This temple was built for him,* she thought. *They are sacrificing those animals because he is going to be sacrificed someday.*

She looked at the questioning faces of the

priests turned toward Jesus and wished she could explain.

But Jesus didn't seem the least bit frustrated. He responded to their questions with a voice as calm and quiet as the night. It held no hint of frustration, only kindness.

Finally the sun began to set, and the shadowy area under the columns grew cold.

"We should go," said Nathan.

Aria nodded and rose to her feet.

Jesus smiled at them. "Safe journey. Peace be with you. I will be here if you need to find me again."

Aria longed to give him a hug, but all the priests and rabbis were watching, so she waved instead.

They walked quietly down the hall of columns to the main gates and passed under the statue of the eagle. As they began walking down the stairs, the sun was setting behind Jerusalem.

"It looks like the sun is melting," said Nathan. And it did—the edge of the sky was filled with a spreading pool of glowing, golden light. It made the ivory towers, walls, and buildings of the old city gleam.

"Jerusalem is shining like gold," said Aria.

10

WHERE IS HE?

Nathan and Aria climbed down the long staircase. The streets were quiet, and most people had gone into their homes for the night. Lights began to flicker on throughout the city. The Roman guards still stood at the turning point of the staircase.

Aria watched them carefully as she walked past. It seemed like they were hardly breathing.

"Short, tall, tall, short," said Nathan. "Why do you think the steps are different sizes? It makes it hard to go fast."

"Maybe they want you to walk slowly when you're going to the temple," said Aria.

"I wouldn't want to fall down these steps!" said Nathan.

At last they reached the bottom. The plaza was empty now.

"Which way?" said Nathan.

Aria didn't answer. She turned her head. "Did you hear that?" she asked. The sound of soft sobs came again.

Nathan nodded.

A couple rounded the corner and entered the plaza. The man had his arm around the woman, who was crying into his shoulder.

"It's all right," the man said gently. "We'll find him."

The woman lifted her face and noticed Nathan and Aria. She wiped her eyes and pointed toward them. They came closer.

Aria could see that the couple's clothes were dusty, and they both looked exhausted.

"Please," the woman said. "We are looking

for our son, Yeshua. He is twelve years old, about this tall," she gestured with her hand, "and is wearing a brown cloak. Have you seen him?"

Aria choked and couldn't reply.

But Nathan nodded eagerly, pointing up the stairs. "We've seen him," he said.

Aria found her voice at last. "He's in the temple," she said, "teaching the priests."

The woman looked shocked. "Teaching? Are you sure?" Her face was kind and beautiful, and she had the same gentle eyes as Jesus.

Nathan and Aria nodded at the same time. "Yes," said Aria. "We're sure."

Mary's face filled with joy, and Joseph smiled. "Thank you so much," he said. "We have been so worried."

Joseph put his arm around Mary, and together they began climbing the steps leading to the temple. Even though they were tired, they climbed quickly, looking at the temple as if it were their only hope.

Nathan and Aria watched them go. Part of Aria wanted to follow them, to be there at the moment when they found him. She imagined Mary's happiness and her response when Jesus explained that he had been about His Father's business.

But instead, Aria turned away. She would let them have that moment alone. Plus, now she could see their faces in her mind, and imagining it was almost as good as seeing the real thing.

11

A NARROW ESCAPE

"That was Mary and Joseph," said Nathan. "We just helped them find Yeshua, I mean, Jesus!"

Aria smiled. "I know! The cool thing about the tunnel is that every time we use it, we find someone to help."

"Jesus told us he was going to stay there in case we needed to find him again," Nathan pointed out. "Do you think he knew we were going to help his parents?"

"Hmm, I wonder," Aria said thoughtfully.

The walls of the old city were dusky and filled with shadows. The streets were deserted, the shops closed up tight.

"We'd better get out the flashlights," said

Nathan. He pulled the headlamps from the scripture bag and clicked them on.

"And the GPS," said Aria. "Or we will never find our way out of this place!"

Nathan unzipped the bag and pulled out the GPS.

"One more thing," said Aria, reaching into the bag. She found a few granola bars and carried them to the spot where the begging man had been sitting.

"What are you doing?" asked Nathan.

"Trying to be like Jesus," said Aria, smiling. She left the granola bars in the corner for the man to find.

"Good idea," said Nathan. He looked at the GPS. "We're here," he said, pointing to a dot on the screen. "Damascus Gate is way over there."

"The streets are like a maze," said Aria.

Nathan nodded. "Then we'd better go!"

Inky shadows filled up the stone streets.

The corners were dark and creepy. A shiver ran down Aria's back, and she walked as fast as she could without tripping.

Stars twinkled in the sky high above them as night descended. Their shoes clicked and clacked on the stones.

They stopped every couple of minutes to check the directions on the GPS. The streets branched off every which way, and nothing looked familiar in the dark.

The next time they paused to check the GPS, they heard a snarling from the shadows behind them.

Aria froze and grabbed Nathan's arm.

A skinny dog emerged from the shadows. The light from their flashlights shone on his long, pointed teeth.

Nathan reached into his bag and grabbed a granola bar. "Here, boy," he said, holding it out and waving it. "Here ya go."

The dog sniffed at the bar but continued to growl and move closer. Nathan dropped the bar in front of the dog and pulled on Aria's arm. "Run!" he said.

They raced down the street, their feet pounding on the stones. The dog chased after them, barking angrily.

"Ahhhh!" screamed Aria. She pumped her arms, trying to ignore the burning in her chest.

The dog seemed to be gaining. He was still barking furiously. The road turned to the right, and they were lost from the dog's view for a few seconds. Thinking quickly, Nathan grabbed Aria's arm and pulled her into a dark, shadowy side street.

"Shhh," he said. Aria clamped her hands over her own mouth to quiet her breathing.

The barking, snarling dog shot past the street where they had turned. He kept running, and the sound of his barking melted into the night.

After a few seconds, Aria took her hand off her mouth and gasped. "Is he gone?"

Nathan peeked around the corner. "I think so," he said.

12

NOT SO FAST

They turned down two more side streets, just to make sure they had really lost the dog.

After the second turn, Aria said, "Look where we are!"

"Damascus Gate!"

The tall spires of the gate shone like a castle under the light of the moon. Nathan and Aria ran toward the gate eagerly.

"Halt!" said a voice. Suddenly a long spear blocked their path. "Who goes there?"

Nathan and Aria skidded to a stop.

A tall Roman soldier with a helmet, shield, sword, and spear stood in front of them.

"Uhhh, it's just us," said Aria.

"What are you doing in the city after dark?" asked the soldier.

"Our names are Nathan and Aria," said Nathan. "We got lost, sir."

"And then we were chased by a dog!" added Aria.

The polished metal of the guard's sword and shield glinted in the moonlight. His eyes were beady, and his face was stern.

"Where are you going?" he asked.

"We don't live far from here," said Nathan. "We're going home."

Aria nodded. She really wanted to be home right now.

"The city is no place for children after dark," said the soldier.

"Yes, sir," said Nathan and Aria together.

"You may go." He waved them off with his hand, but he continued to watch as they walked away.

Nathan and Aria walked across the plaza that had been filled with people. It was empty now. They climbed the stone steps and headed toward the spot where the enchanted tunnel had been.

Aria glanced back at the Roman soldier. He was still watching them suspiciously.

"He isn't going to believe we live in here!" she said.

"Don't look at him," said Nathan. "By the time he tries to follow us, we'll be gone."

"I wonder if he could get through the tunnel," said Aria. "What would Mom say if we brought a Roman soldier home for dinner?"

Nathan laughed. He pulled the pioneer bonnet out of his scripture bag and handed it to his sister.

Aria tied the bonnet on her head, and they used their flashlights to find the narrow opening in the rock.

Their flashlights threw strange shadows on the walls of the tunnel. Aria shivered. She knelt down and started to crawl. An electric sizzle passed through the tunnel, and soon the ground felt cold and smooth beneath their hands.

13

HOME AGAIN

"There's the door," said Nathan, pointing at the glimmer of light ahead.

Aria reached it first. She pushed open the door and they tumbled into the gym—right onto someone's feet! It was Brother DeLeon, the Young Men president.

"Nathan? Aria?" he said. "What on earth are you two doing?"

"Ummm," said Aria.

"Errrr," said Nathan.

He looked at their dusty costumes with a confused expression on his face.

"Does your mother know you are here?"

"Yes," said Aria. She was trying desperately to think of what she could tell him that would be the truth. "We, umm, just needed something out of the storage cupboard."

"Besides the chairs?" said Brother DeLeon.

"Yeah," said Nathan. "But we'll put them back now—we promise!"

Brother DeLeon looked as though he wasn't sure if he should be upset or not. He looked from Nathan to Aria, then back again. "That's good," said Brother DeLeon, "because we're going to play basketball now."

"Sorry about that," said Aria.

Together they pushed the heavy rack of chairs back into the tunnel. It was much easier with Brother DeLeon helping.

"Thanks, Brother DeLeon," said Aria. "We'd better go now!"

"No problem," said Brother DeLeon. He scratched his head as they hopped up on the stage. Aria picked up the new bonnet she had left lying there and added it to the box of church costumes.

The children grabbed their regular clothes and headed toward the restrooms to change.

"He thinks we're crazy!" Aria whispered.

Nathan snickered.

14

NOW IT MAKES SENSE

Back at home, the children stashed their tunnel costumes in Aria's closet.

Mom stopped at the door to Aria's room and looked the children over. She seemed surprised and relieved that their clothes still looked clean. "Hey," she said, with a smile. "You two better get started on your homework. We're going to have dinner soon."

"Okay," said Nathan. Mom left the room.

"Dinner," said Aria. "I'm starving!"

"I guess we forgot to eat," said Nathan. He handed Aria a granola bar and bit into one himself.

"You? Forget about food?" said Aria. "I don't believe it!"

"I could definitely go for some pita bread right about now!"

"Me too!" said Aria. She took the orange and gold scarf out of the scripture bag and wound it around her hair. "Look, I'm ready to go back to Old Jerusalem."

"Let's get going on our homework," said Nathan.

"Okay!" said Aria. She unwound the scarf, folded it, and placed it on her shelf next to a blue scarab ring and some Indian beads.

"Is it okay if we use the computer, Mom?" Nathan called.

"For a few minutes," she called back.

They hurried to the kitchen and turned on the computer. Their mom was busy adding ingredients to several pans on the stove. Aria typed in "Jerusalem temple." Thousands of articles came up. She clicked on one and an artist's drawing of the temple filled the screen.

The temple was white and gold with a spiral of smoke in front.

"That's it!" said Nathan quietly, so their mother wouldn't hear. "That's where we were today."

Aria read, "The first temple in Jerusalem was built by King Solomon. This temple was destroyed, but it was later rebuilt by King Herod. It became famous for its white marble walls that shone in the sun. Animal sacrifices were offered on the altar, and the smoke rising to heaven represented the prayers of the people rising to God."

"Wow," said Nathan. "I want to go back to Jerusalem someday and see it again!"

Aria kept reading. "Jesus taught at the temple when he was twelve years old. And later he drove out the moneychangers. The temple was destroyed by the Romans in A.D. 70. The soldiers threw torches into the building and knocked down the columns."

"Really?" said Nathan. "I can't believe anyone would do that."

Aria nodded. "People burned the Nauvoo temple too."

"Oh, yeah," said Nathan. "I forgot. I guess that means we can't go back. Hey, what were those black boxes everyone was wearing?"

Aria looked through the articles and found one on clothing. "In the temple, men wore white prayer shawls and black boxes on their foreheads and arms. The boxes were called *tefillin*. Inside the box was a small scroll with the words from Deuteronomy 6:4–5: 'Hear, O Israel: the Lord our God is one Lord. And thou shalt love the Lord thy God with all thine heart, and with all thy soul, and with all thy might.'"

"Hey," said Nathan. "That's what Jesus said was the most important commandment."

Aria nodded.

"Look," said Aria, "this article says that Jesus taught in the temple in a place called the Porticoes—a long hallway lined with columns."

Nathan read over her shoulder. "No one knows what Jesus and the teachers were discussing. Perhaps they talked about the Passover festival, the temple sacrifices, or the best way to serve God. All who heard him were amazed by his understanding."

"No one knows what Jesus taught," said Aria.

"Unless they have an enchanted tunnel," said Nathan.

"Time for dinner!" Mom said.

"Okay!" said Nathan and Aria.

They closed the computer window and

went to wash their hands. "I can't wait to tell Brother King about our latest 'research,'" said Nathan.

"He's going to be very surprised that you know so much about Jerusalem," said Aria.

"Yep," said Nathan. "But I don't think I'll be able to bring him the book I used to study!"

"Maybe next time," said Aria with a smile.

EPILOGUE

According to the book of Luke, Jesus and his parents journeyed to Jerusalem to celebrate the Passover feast. During this feast, thousands of pilgrims flooded the holy city. The festival lasted for a week, during which only unleavened bread was eaten. Worshippers brought lambs to the temple to be sacrificed. Then they ate the cooked lamb with bitter herbs and matzah bread and recounted the story of the Exodus.

The journey from Jerusalem to Nazareth was seventy miles and lasted several days. People usually traveled by caravan with a large group of family and friends. This is why it took Mary and Joseph a whole day to realize that

Jesus was missing—they probably thought that he was with others of their group. After seeking him among family and friends without success, they turned back to Jerusalem to look for him. The city is large and complex, with a maze of streets that would have been filled with worshippers preparing to return home. Three days after they realized he was missing, they finally found him in the temple.

At the age of twelve, Jesus would have been preparing for his bar mitzvah, the time when a Jewish boy would begin to wear *tefillin* and read the scriptures in the synagogue. He would then become a "son of the commandment." It was the custom for priests, Pharisees, and other Jewish religious leaders to gather before the evening sacrifice in the area known as the Porticoes. They gathered together to discuss the scriptures. People knew that they could come to seek religious guidance from the teachers. It would not have been unusual for a boy like Jesus to sit among them, asking questions.

But Luke says that "all that heard him were astonished at his understanding and answers" (Luke 2:47). Clearly they recognized that the Savior had an extremely unusual and unique grasp of the religious concepts of the day.

The scriptures do not tell us what topics were being discussed. However, it seems likely that they may have been discussing the Passover festival that had been recently celebrated, or the purpose of the sacrifices, which were performed on the altar only a short distance away from where they sat. The question of the greatest commandment was also a commonly discussed topic, and one that was asked of the Savior later in his ministry (Mark 12:28).

We also do not know what Jesus was doing

during the three days that Mary and Joseph sought him. However, the Savior's life was spent doing good and ministering to those who were less fortunate. Therefore, it seems likely that during some of that time he perhaps served those who were suffering.

When Mary and Joseph at last found Jesus and asked him why he had stayed behind, Jesus replied, "How is it that ye sought me? Wist ye not that I must be about my Father's business?" (Luke 2:49). From a very young age, the Savior was concerned with doing his Father's will. It was to be the main focus of the rest of his life, as well as the motivation for his atoning sacrifice.

FUN FACTS

Yeshua: Jesus' name in Hebrew is Yeshua. It means "salvation."

Tefillin: The black boxes used by Jews for prayer, also called phylacteries, are worn on the forehead and the arm. Inside the box, important scriptures are written on tiny scrolls, including Deuteronomy 6:4–9.

Children of Israel: The majority of members of The Church of Jesus Christ of Latter-day Saints are descendants of Israel through the tribe of Ephraim. Those who are not literal descendants are adopted into the house of Israel at baptism.

Jerusalem Temple: In order to make the Jews happy, King Herod rebuilt the temple in

Jerusalem. It was a massive project that took forty-six years! But when it was finished, the temple was one of the wonders of the ancient world. The Talmud says, "He who has not seen the Temple of Herod, has never seen a beautiful building" (Babylonian Talmud, Baba Batra, 4a; Shemot Rabba 36:1). It was covered with white marble and gold. Herod placed a golden eagle over the main temple gates. This made the Jews very angry, since having "no graven images" was one of the Ten Commandments.

In the time of Jesus, the land of Israel was controlled by the Roman Empire. Jews were waiting for a messiah who would help them regain their freedom. During the feasts, many Roman guards were sent to the city in order to make sure the Jews didn't revolt.

During Jesus' life, he prophesied that the temple would be destroyed. In A.D. 70, the Romans besieged Jerusalem and set fire to the holy temple. The Jews were scattered, and the temple was never rebuilt. An impressive Muslim mosque—called "The Dome of the Rock"—was later built in its place. The scriptures say that before the Millennium a temple will once again be built in Jerusalem.

The temple was called the "Mountain of the Lord" and was built at the top of a hill. Huge flights of steps led to the temple, and more steps inside led to the Holy of Holies. This represented a person's journey closer to God. The steps were different heights on purpose so that people approaching the temple were forced to walk slowly. Many modern temples today are also built on the tops of hills.

Jerusalem: The Old City of Jerusalem is still a labyrinth of stone streets filled with shops and shopkeepers. It is possible today to stand in sacred places where Jesus once walked.

TO LEARN MORE

You can learn more about Jerusalem by reading these books yourself or by asking a parent or teacher to help you:

Peter Connolly, *Living in the Time of Jesus of Nazareth* (Tel Aviv: Steimatzky, 1983).

William J. Hamblin and David Rolph Seely, *Solomon's Temple: Myth and History* (New York: Thames and Hudson, 2007).

Jenny Roberts, *Bible Then and Now* (New York: Macmillan, 1996).

RECIPE FOR PITA BREAD

1 tablespoon yeast
1 teaspoon sugar
1¼ cups warm water
¼ teaspoon salt
4 cups flour

Dissolve the yeast and sugar in the water until the yeast is foamy (about 10 minutes). Mix the salt with two cups of flour and add to the yeast mixture. Beat for five minutes and then add the rest of the flour. Let dough rise for 30 minutes. Divide dough into balls and roll out as thin as possible. Let rise another 30 minutes. Bake in a 500-degree F. oven for about 5 minutes or until the rounds puff up and begin to turn golden.

ABOUT THE AUTHOR

Marianne Monson spent much of her childhood looking for magic passageways. Reading good books has always been one of her favorite adventures. She studied English at Brigham Young University and also spent a semester in Jerusalem, where she walked through Hezekiah's Tunnel. Now, she particularly enjoys following her children, Nathan and Aria, as they discover their own enchanted tunnels.

Marianne holds an MFA from Vermont College in writing for children and young adults. She teaches creative writing at Portland Community College and serves as a Gospel Doctrine teacher in her ward in Hillsboro, Oregon. You can visit her at www.mariannemonson.com.